BRAVE MAEVE

A Story to Help Young Children and Grown-Ups Navigate COVID-19

ROXY LEESON AND KATIE LEESON

Illustrated by Nick Hausman

AuthorHouse™
1663 Liberty Drive
Bloomington, IN 47403
www.authorhouse.com
Phone: 833-262-8899

Because of the dynamic nature of the Internet, any web addresses or links contained in this book may have changed
since publication and may no longer be valid. The views expressed in this work are solely those of the authors and do
not necessarily reflect the views of the publisher, and the publisher hereby disclaims any responsibility for them.

Any people depicted in stock imagery provided by Getty Images are models,
and such images are being used for illustrative purposes only.
Certain stock imagery © Getty Images.

This book is printed on acid-free paper.

ISBN: 978-1-6655-1196-4 (sc)
ISBN: 978-1-6655-1197-1 (e)

Library of Congress Control Number: 2020925656

Print information available on the last page.

Published by AuthorHouse 01/14/2021

authorHOUSE®

To our brave Maeve.
To Will, Kate, and Jess.

My name is Maeve. What's your name? I live in a yellow house with my mom and my favorite stuffed animal, Margaret. What color is your home? I'm four years old. How old are you?

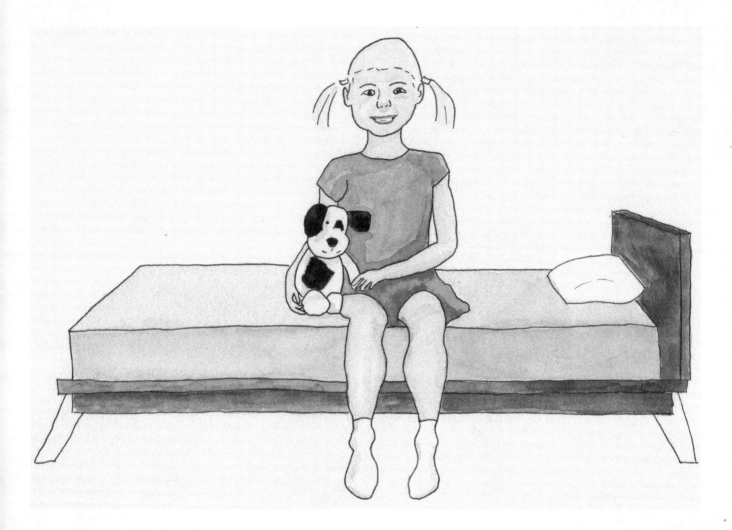

My favorite color is purple. What's yours? I love bugs, especially purple ones if I can find them. I like to ride my bike, play hide and seek, go to the playground, take care of Margaret, roll down hills, do art projects, wear PJs, dance, and so much more! What do you like to do?

Last fall when I was three and the trees started to change colors, I went to school for the first time with lots of other children.

We did so many fun things together and I got to wear my butterfly backpack every day.

In the winter, when snow covered the playground, we all stayed home for a holiday vacation.

We came back to school in January and everyone cheered, "Happy New Year!"

One day at the end of winter, just before the trees started to grow new leaves again, my mom told me that I wouldn't be going to school for a while, but it wasn't a holiday vacation.

She said there was something really, really small called a germ floating in the air that could make us feel sick. The germ is called a coronavirus. This one is called COVID-19. Those are funny names.

To keep everyone away from the germs, my mom said we would be staying home for a while. If there are lots of germs in lots of places, it's called a pandemic. When my great grandfather was my age he had to stay home too because there was a different pandemic.

My mom didn't know how long we would stay at home, but said lots of people were working very hard to keep us safe like:

- doctors, nurses, and scientists;
- police officers and firefighters;
- grocery store workers; and
- delivery truck drivers.

I felt so grateful for all these people. Can you think of anyone else who helped you?

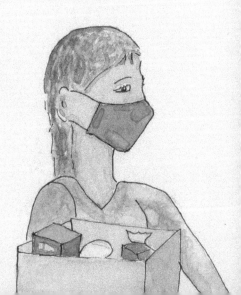

While I stayed at home, I couldn't:

- have playdates or see my friends;
- play at the playground;
- go to ballet or gym classes;
- hug and play with my grandmother and grandfather; or
- have my babysitter come to my house.

When I went outside, I had to wear a mask that covered my nose and mouth. It made me talk funny and look different. I got used to the mask, but I missed the way we used to do things.

We stayed at home a lot. My mom didn't go to her office. She was on her phone and computer at home all the time, but that's what she had to do. Even Margaret wondered why we were around the house so much.

Some fun things happened while we were at home, too:

- We drove by peoples' houses and honked our horns on their birthdays.
- I saw my friends and classmates on the computer instead of at school.
- My mom and I started a vegetable garden. It was filled with bugs!

My mom, Margaret, and I cooked a lot together and had pretend parties. We did science experiments, made costumes, and of course, danced.

When the tomatoes in my new garden started to grow, I had to say goodbye to my teachers through the computer.

My camp was canceled, and the town pool didn't open for the summer.

I heard my mom talk a lot about the germs and when they'd go away. I felt sad sometimes. We were all a little sad. How did you feel?

In the Fall, I went back to my school. It's a little different, but still lots of fun and I know that everyone is working really hard to keep you, me, and Margaret safe and happy until COVID-19 goes away!

17

CPSIA information can be obtained
at www.ICGtesting.com
Printed in the USA
BVHW021616100221
599765BV00006B/69